W9-CSH-311

DATE DUE

FEB 1 2 2014		
GAYLORD		PRINTED IN U.S.A.

AFRICA FOCUS

CHANGING AFRICA

Rob Bowden and Rosie Wilson

Heinemann Library
Chicago, Illinois

www.heinemannraintree.com
Visit our website to find out
more information about
Heinemann-Raintree books.

To order:

☎ Phone 888-454-2279

💻 Visit www.heinemannraintree.com
to browse our catalog and order online.

©2010 Heinemann Library
an imprint of Capstone Global Library, LLC
Chicago, Illinois

Edited by Louise Galpine and Rachel Howells
Designed by Richard Parker and Manhattan Design
Original illustrations © Capstone Global Library Ltd
Illustrated by Oxford Designers and Illustrators
Picture research by Mica Brancic
Originated by Heinemann Library
Printed in China by Leo Paper Products Ltd.

14 13 12 11 10
10 9 8 7 6 5 4 3 2 1

Library of Congress Cataloging-in-Publication Data
Bowden, Rob, 1973-
  Changing Africa / Rob Bowden and Rosie Wilson.
    p. cm. -- (Africa focus)
  Includes bibliographical references and index.
  ISBN 978-1-4329-2437-9 (hc) -- ISBN 978-1-4329-2442-3
(pb)
  1. Africa--Social conditions--21st century. 2. Africa--
Economic conditions--21st century. I. Wilson, Rosie. II. Title.
  HN773.5.B68 2008
  306.096'090511--dc22
                        2008048277

Acknowledgments

We would like to thank the following for permission to
reproduce photographs: Corbis pp. **4** (Lynsey Addario), **7 &
12** (© Louise Gubb), **11 & 13** (© Gideon Mendel), **19 & 22**
(© Andy Aitchison), **23** (© George Steinmetz), **25** (© Martin
Harvey), **31** (epa/ © Salvatore Di Nolfi), **32** (© Wendy Stone),
33 (© Liba Taylor), **39** (© Charles & Josette Lenars), **40** (©
Jenny Mayfield/ YouthAids/Reuters), **41** (epa/ © Gero Breloer);
EASI-Images p. **15** (Rob Bowden); Getty Images pp. **5** (Gallo
Images/ David Bloomer), **9** (Marco Longari/ © AFP), **24**
(AFP/ Gregoire Pourtier), **26** (Behrouz Mehri/ © AFP), **28**
(Issouf Sanogo/ © AFP), **35** (Ramzi Haidar/ © AFP); © Getty
Images News p. **36** (Christopher Furlong); Photolibrary pp.
16 (Imagestate RM/ Piers Cavendish), **18** (David Reed), **21**
(Sylvain Grandadam).

Cover photograph of Nigerian pupils working on computers,
Abuja, reproduced with permission of Reuters (Afolabi
Sotunde).

We would like to thank Danny Block for his invaluable help in
the preparation of this book.

Contents

Some words are printed in bold, **like this**. You can find out what they mean by looking in the glossary on page 44.

Africa in the 21st Century

Africa today faces many challenges. The **continent** is struggling to fight the spread of **HIV/AIDS**, a fatal condition with no cure. In 2007 there were about 22 million Africans **infected** with the disease. In the Democratic Republic of the Congo, Sudan, and other African countries, wars continue and threaten peace in the wider region. Another recent challenge is **climate change**. Climate experts believe Africa could be one of the world's worst affected regions. Scientists have warned of greater risk of **drought** and **famine** because of less predictable weather patterns.

But the biggest challenge of all is poverty. Africa is the world's poorest continent, and this is made worse by its fast-growing population.

A victim is carried to safety by an **African Union (AU)** soldier in Darfur, Sudan. Fighting in Darfur is one of Africa's biggest challenges at the start of the 21st century. Many innocent people have been injured, killed, or forced from their homes.

Opportunities

But there is hope, too. Many African **economies** are growing steadily for the first time since the early 1970s. The **international community** has made new agreements to help Africa reduce poverty. These include cancelling the **debts** of Africa's poorest countries. This allows them to spend money on their own development instead of paying back wealthier nations. New **trade** opportunities with China, India, and within Africa are also reasons to be positive about the future.

The shadow of history

For much of the 1900s, European nations controlled most of Africa as **colonies**. They took control of Africa's best farmland and used it for growing tea, sugar, coffee, cocoa, cotton, rubber, peanuts, and spices, all to be sent back to Europe. The Europeans also controlled Africa's most precious resources, including copper, gold, and diamonds. Although the colonizers valued Africa's resources, they did not take care of its people. Most Africans were kept in low-skilled, low-paid jobs.

During the second half of the 1900s, African countries became **independent** of their colonizers, starting with Ghana when it became independent from the UK in 1957. This freed them from European control, but by then patterns of trade, landownership, and political control were established. In many parts of the continent, these patterns remain largely unchanged today.

A woman shops at a mall in Cape Town, South Africa. A growing number of Africans have enough money to enjoy lifestyles similar to those of people in Europe or the United States.

5

Signs of change

By the beginning of the 21st century, many African countries were showing signs of escaping from the shadows of **colonial** life. Peace had returned to countries such as Uganda and Sierra Leone that had suffered years of **civil war**. Economies were changing to produce more than just **raw materials**, and more people had access to schools and hospitals than ever before. However, this change and progress is not evenly spread across the continent.

North African countries such as Tunisia, Morocco, and Libya achieved much greater progress than countries south of the Sahara Desert such as Ghana and Kenya. Some countries such as Zambia achieved no progress at all by measures such as **life expectancy** (see table). In fact, life expectancy there is lower now than 45 years ago, mainly due to the spread of HIV/AIDS.

Country	Life expectancy (years)		Average yearly income per person ($)	
	1960	2005	1965	2005
Egypt	46	71	160	1,270
Morocco	47	70	220	1,990
Libya	47	74	810	5,870
Algeria	47	72	260	2,720
Tunisia	49	73	230	2,870
Ghana	46	59	220	440
Senegal	41	62	250	740
Kenya	47	53	100	530
Zambia	45	41	260	500

Source: World Development Indicators, 2008

Keeping up

Even though Africa has progressed, the rest of the world is progressing faster. Africa is being left behind. One way to show this is to look at the average life expectancy of children born in 2000. If they were born in the United States or Europe, they could expect to live until 2075. Children born in Asia would survive until around 2067, but if they were born in Africa then they would be lucky to live beyond 2049. This is partly due to the devastating impact of HIV/AIDS in Africa, but it also shows Africa's struggle to keep up with development in the rest of the world. Africa is changing rapidly, but what the future holds for Africa is still uncertain.

Students take a business exam at a college in Johannesburg, South Africa. Many colleges offer classes to improve the skills of the population.

AFRICA ON THE MOVE

"Africa today is a continent on the move, making ... progress on delivering better health, education, growth, trade, and poverty-reduction outcomes."
Dr. Gobind Nankani, former World Bank vice-president for Africa

Changing Lives

Africa's population more than tripled during the second half of the 1900s. By 1999 it had reached 767 million people and was the fastest-growing population in the world. The rate of growth is slowing down, but in 2007 the population passed 945 million. By 2050 it is expected to double to more than 1.9 billion!

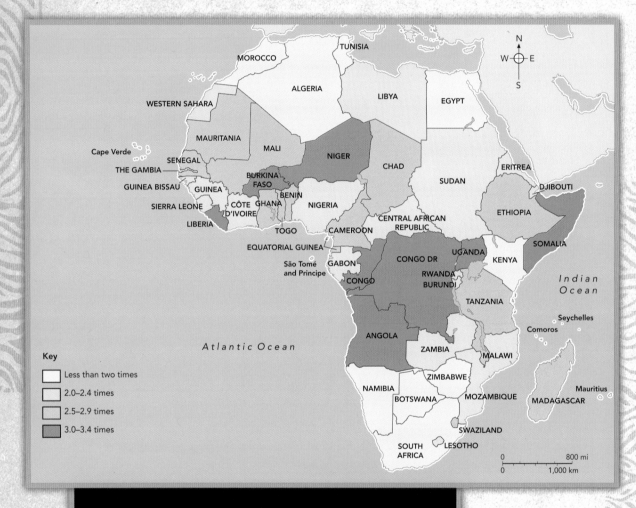

Key
- Less than two times
- 2.0–2.4 times
- 2.5–2.9 times
- 3.0–3.4 times

This map shows by how much Africa's populations are expected to increase by 2050.

AFRICA FACT

Nigeria is the most populated country in Africa. In 2007 at least one in every seven Africans was a Nigerian.

On the move

Every year more and more Africans are leaving **rural** areas to live in cities. This is normally because of land shortages in rural areas, or because people hope to find higher-paid work in the cities.

Between 1985 and 2005, the number of Africans living in towns and cities more than doubled, to 349 million. Despite this, less than half of Africa's population lives in **urban** areas. This makes it the least urban region of the world. This is changing though, and by 2030 Africa is expected to become more urban than rural. By 2050 experts predict that 62 percent of Africans will live in towns and cities.

Providing homes for Africa's fast-growing urban population is a major challenge. Many people have to live in **slums** such as Kibera in Nairobi, Kenya. At least 200 million Africans live in slums. Some slums have populations of more than half a million people!

LIFE IN THE SLUMS

"Kiberans live in tin shacks or mud houses with no toilets, no beds, and little water. Electricity is almost nonexistent. Most of the **pit latrines** are full, so people use 'flying toilets' where they excrete [go to the toilet] into plastic bags and throw them in piles on the street."
United Nations, State of World Population, 2007

Residents of Kibera slum in Nairobi walk along one of its narrow paths. The basic buildings and waste problems can be seen behind them.

Meeting basic needs

Across Africa, millions of people do not have access to basic needs such as safe water and electricity. Proper toilets and secure, healthy homes are also in short supply in many areas. In general, people in North Africa have better living conditions than people in **sub-Saharan Africa**. Living conditions are also normally better in urban areas than in rural areas.

Country	Access to safe water (% of population)	
	Urban	Rural
North Africa		
Egypt	99	97
Algeria	88	80
Morocco	99	56
Sub-Saharan Africa		
Kenya	83	46
Nigeria	67	31
Mozambique	72	26

Improving conditions

Living standards are improving in many parts of Africa. In South Africa, the government is building millions of new homes across the country. These homes are basic, but give people access to water, toilets, electricity, and waste collection. In Egypt, the government is building new cities to improve living conditions, but many of Egypt's poorest people cannot afford to live in them. Low-cost solutions are also being introduced across Africa. These include basic pit latrines that provide safe and sanitary toilets. Educating people about things such as how to make water safe for drinking is another simple way to improve people's lives.

Feeding Africa

Although Africa has some of the world's most **fertile** farmland, large parts of the **continent** suffer from food shortages. Much of the best farmland is used to produce **crops** for **export**. Food supplies are also badly affected by conflicts if farmers are forced to abandon their land. **Drought** is another cause of food shortages, as are rising food prices. Often farmers have no crops left and can only feed the remains of the plants to their animals.

In 2008, parts of Ethiopia, Somalia, Kenya, Uganda, and Djibouti suffered their worst droughts in more than 20 years, and 17.5 million people were at risk from starvation.

Water is a basic need that many people in Africa are missing. Improved water pumps like this one in Kenya provide people with clean and healthy water and help to reduce the risk of diseases.

Killer diseases

One of the greatest challenges facing Africa in the 21st century is the impact of two killer diseases—**malaria** and **HIV/AIDS**.

Malaria

Malaria is passed to humans when a mosquito carrying the disease bites them. People can take antimalarial drugs to try and prevent them catching malaria, but these do not always work. They are also too expensive for many people. A better solution is to reduce the chances of being bitten. Mosquitoes are most active at night, and so sleeping under a mosquito net is one of the best ways to do this.

"Roll Back Malaria"

There are around 365 million cases of malaria reported in Africa every year, and almost one million deaths. "Roll Back Malaria" is an international campaign to reduce malaria around the world. In Africa, the campaign will provide 300 million mosquito nets by 2010. In 2006 only around 72 million nets were being used in Africa.

These two children in Ethiopia are reading beneath a mosquito net, which covers the bed and protects them from being bitten and infected with malaria.

People infected with HIV march in Eastern Cape, South Africa. The march was part of World AIDS Day activities, to make people more aware of the disease.

HIV/AIDS

Human Immunodeficiency Virus (HIV) is passed between people through unsafe sex or **infected** blood. There is no cure for HIV, but special drugs can help to delay HIV from becoming AIDS (Acquired Immunodeficiency Syndrome). AIDS is **fatal** and killed around 1.5 million people in Africa in 2007.

The drugs that can keep HIV patients healthy are called **antiretroviral (ARV)** drugs. They were first produced by Western drug companies and were very expensive. Many African countries could not afford them. Today, the drug companies have allowed others to produce ARVs under special licenses. This has lowered the cost of ARVs a lot and given millions of HIV patients in Africa the chance to live a longer life.

AFRICA FACT

Many children in Africa have lost one or both parents to HIV/AIDS. In 2007 there were as many as 15 million AIDS orphans living in Africa.

Educating for change

Millions of Africans have never been to school and around one-third of Africans over 15 years of age cannot read or write. In countries such as Burkina Faso and Chad, as many as 75 percent of the population cannot read or write. Improving education is one of Africa's greatest challenges. People who are better educated are more aware of how to keep themselves and their family healthy. They have better diets and fewer illnesses than less educated people. They also often choose to have smaller families. Better education could also help with Africa's other problems, such as the spread of disease and population growth.

Universal Primary Education (UPE)

In 1996 the Ugandan government made elementary school free for up to four children in every family. Within a few months, the number of children in elementary school increased from around three million to more than five million. Many schools were so crowded that classes had to be held outside, under trees. Thousands of new schools have since been built, and the number of teachers has almost doubled.

	Before UPE (1996)	After UPE (2003)
Children in elementary school	3.1 million	7.6 million
Number of elementary schools	8,531	13,353
Number of elementary school teachers	81,564	145,587

This table shows the impact of Universal Primary Education (UPE) in Uganda.

Changing families

Family life in Africa is changing quickly in the 21st century. More people are living away from their families because they need to find work in towns and cities. Others have left home to study. These changes mean that people are marrying later and having fewer children than their parents. Divorce and separated families are also becoming more common.

In southern Africa, many families have been badly affected by HIV/AIDS. In some families both the parents have died, leaving their children to be cared for by grandparents or other relatives. Many children themselves have become carers, taking care of their sick parents or caring for brothers and sisters because their parents are too ill to take care of them.

This school is on the edge of Kampala, Uganda. It shows how crowded classrooms have become since UPE. The building and teachers are paid for by the government, but parents must buy uniforms, books, and school supplies.

Earning a Living

Africa is the poorest continent in the world, but the true picture of poverty in Africa is more complicated. Some countries are much wealthier than others. Patterns of poverty are also changing. Equatorial Guinea, for example, began **exporting** oil in 1995 and this led to a rapid increase in its wealth. In 1995 Equatorial Guinea had an average **income** of just $410 per person, but by 2007 this had increased to $12,860 per person.

The wealth of a country does not tell the full story, though. The way wealth is shared is just as important for reducing poverty.

Sharing the wealth

In many African countries, wealth is shared unevenly. In Lesotho, for example, the wealthiest 10 percent of the population share almost half of the country's wealth, while the poorest 10 percent share less than one percent of it. This difference in wealth is known as inequality.

In several countries, inequality has been linked to a rise in crime. In South Africa and Kenya, many wealthy people now feel so in danger that they live in houses protected by high fences and armed guards. Even driving can be dangerous. Carjacking—when someone steals a car while someone else is using it—is now a common crime in South Africa. The South African police recorded more than 14,000 cases of carjacking from 2007 to 2008.

There are enormous divides between the lives of the rich and the poor in Africa. These inequalities are greatest in cities such as Kampala, Uganda, where basic housing can be found alongside modern city skyscrapers.

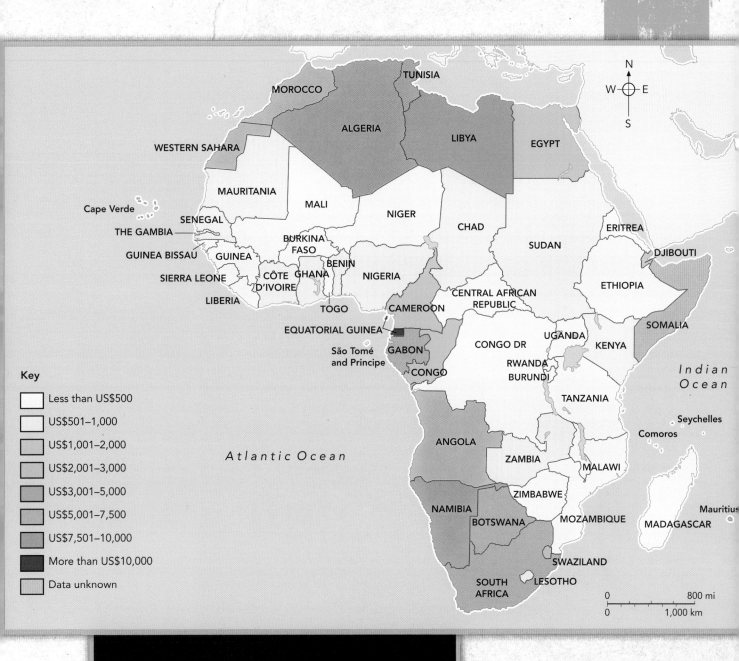

Key

	Less than US$500
	US$501–1,000
	US$1,001–2,000
	US$2,001–3,000
	US$3,001–5,000
	US$5,001–7,500
	US$7,501–10,000
	More than US$10,000
	Data unknown

This map shows the average wealth (in $ per year) of people living in Africa in 2007. It shows there is a wide range in wealth across the continent.

Trapped in poverty

During the **colonial** period, African countries were prevented from developing their own industries. Instead, they were used to provide **raw materials**, such as minerals and agricultural products for industries in Europe. Many African countries still rely on the export of raw materials for their income today, but the price of many raw materials has been falling. This means that each year Africa is getting less for what it produces. At the same time, Africa is having to pay the same, or more, for **importing** what it consumes. This keeps Africa trapped in poverty and unable to develop its own industries.

A woman picking tea leaves on a tea estate in Zimbabwe. Tea is an important crop in Africa, but it is not very valuable and prices vary greatly year by year.

Unfair trade

The world trade system is unfair to many African farmers. A good example of this is cotton. Cotton farmers in Benin and Burkina Faso produce cotton for much less money than farmers in the United States, but American farmers can still sell cotton for a lower price in world markets. They can do this because the US government gives its cotton farmers money known as a **subsidy** to grow cotton. Because they have this extra money, American farmers can afford to sell their cotton at a lower price than farmers in Africa, who get no subsidy from their governments.

Making trade fair

Fair-trade organizations are working to improve the lives and opportunities of African farmers. They do this by paying them a guaranteed price that is above the normal market price. This allows farmers to **invest** in better health care and education for their families, to improve their farms, or start new businesses. A wide range of fair-trade products now come from Africa (see table below), and hundreds of thousands of farmers have benefited from the scheme.

What is it?	Where is it from?	What does the money do?
Oranges	South Africa	Funds a scheme to make sure black people have equal access to work and training opportunities
Chocolate	Cocoa from Ghana	Develops a large business of 48,000 farmers who vote to decide how the business should grow
Peanuts	Mozambique	Pays workers 25 percent more than local **wage** levels
Sugar	Malawi	Builds new houses and buys medicine for communities

These are some Fair Trade Certified products from Africa that you can buy today in the United States.

A farmer stands with his coffee after cycling to a weighing station where it is weighed and he is paid. He is part of a fair-trade program that helps coffee farmers in Uganda.

Brain drain

A shortage of well-paid jobs for skilled workers means that many of Africa's most skilled people leave to find work elsewhere. This is known as a **brain drain**. Around one-third of Africa's highly-skilled workers, for example doctors, **engineers**, teachers, and scientists, live and work outside of Africa. They are mainly found in Brazil, the United States, Canada, and Europe. Most of them will send money, called **remittances**, back to their families in Africa.

In 2007, around $11 billion was sent to **sub-Saharan African** countries in remittance payments. Ghana alone received $2 billion, equivalent to about one-seventh of its total income in 2007. Though this money benefits Africa, many believe that Africa would benefit even more if the skilled labour stayed in Africa in the first place.

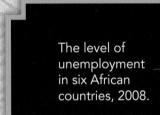

The level of unemployment in six African countries, 2008.

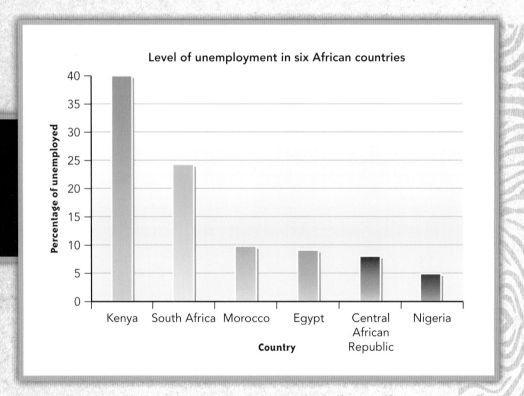

Informal economy

In several African countries, unemployment is a serious problem—sometimes more than a quarter of the population has no job (see graph above). One result of this is a very large **informal economy**. This is where people work unofficially and do not pay **taxes**. Selling things on the side of the street and providing services such as shoe repairs, cleaning, or hairdressing, are common examples of informal jobs. In Tanzania, it is estimated that the informal economy accounts for around half of all economic activity.

AFRICA FACT

Chicago, Illinois, has more Ethiopian doctors working in its hospitals than there are doctors in the country of Ethiopia.

This captain rents his boat to tourists who want to go fishing in Senegal. It is an example of new opportunities in tourism.

New opportunities

Tourism is providing Africa with new opportunities to earn money and create jobs. In 1990 Africa had 15.2 million tourists, with most visiting North-African countries. By 2007 the number of tourists had grown to 44.4 million, and most were now visiting countries in sub-Saharan Africa. The most popular countries to visit include South Africa, Morocco, Tunisia, Kenya, and Botswana.

Changing Environments

Many Africans rely on the environment for their day-to-day survival. They use it to produce food, to grow **crops** for sale, to keep **livestock**, and to collect water for drinking and wood for fuel. They may also hunt animals or gather wild foods such as nuts, berries, leaves, and roots. Because they depend on their environment, Africans have traditionally been very good environmental managers. One way they did this was to change the land they farmed every few years, so that it had time to rest. This would protect the soils and stop them from losing their fertility.

Across much of Africa, women and children spend many hours farming the land and are often expert managers of their environment.

Under threat

Population growth means that more and more land is being used for farming, building, and roads. There is no longer space for farmers to rest their land and move to a new area. Instead, they add chemicals to the soil in order to keep it **fertile**.

Africa's growing population is also putting pressure on water supplies and forests. Many forests have been cleared to make room for farmland or provide wood for fuel. Once the trees are removed, the soil is at risk of **erosion** from wind and rainfall. In Ethiopia, **deforestation** has resulted in the loss of around one billion tons of soil every year because of increased erosion. In addition, more and more of Ethiopia's land is becoming desertlike due to a process called **desertification**.

This photograph shows how the desert is creeping into the town of Tekenket, Mautritania (right). Across Africa deserts are growing, threatening farming and entire villages.

Turning the land to desert

"The risks of desertification are substantial and clear. It contributes to food insecurity, **famine**, and poverty, and can give rise to social, economic, and political tensions."
Secretary-General of the United Nations Kofi Annan, speaking on the UN's World Day to Combat Desertification and Drought, June 17, 2004

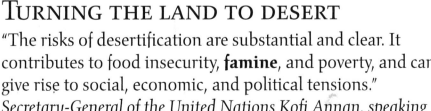

Mining and forestry

Forestry is an important industry in Africa, but it has led to the destruction of many of Africa's best forests. The tropical **rain forests** of West Africa and Central Africa have suffered heavy deforestation for more than 50 years. Nigeria has very little forest left, and countries such as Burundi and Rwanda are losing their forests very quickly.

Forests are sometimes cleared to get to the minerals that lie deep beneath them. Deforestation has increased in the Democratic Republic of the Congo because of mining for columbite-tantalite (CT). CT is a mineral used to make electronic parts for mobile phones, computers, and games consoles. About 80 percent of the world's CT is found in the Democratic Republic of the Congo.

Deforestation in Madagascar has destroyed large areas of forest. The soil becomes unfit for farming and so cleared land is often simply abandoned.

AFRICA FACT

Africa is losing its forests faster than any other region of the world. Around 0.8 percent of its forests are being destroyed every year.

Wildlife loss

Human activity in Africa has led to the loss of many natural **habitats**. Many **species** of birds and animals are now under threat. There are now only a few hundred mountain gorillas living in small sections of Rwanda, Uganda, and the Democratic Republic of the Congo. Elephants, rhinoceros, and large cats such as the cheetah and leopard are also under threat, as well as many smaller animals.

One of the most successful rhinoceros conservation projects has been in Nakuru National Park in Kenya. An electrified fence has been placed around the park to protect the black rhinos from poachers.

RHINOS IN DANGER

Africa has black and white rhinoceros, and both have been badly affected by hunting and **poaching**. In 1984 southern Africa had only 15 white rhinoceros, and the black rhino was almost wiped out completely. A major **conservation** program has since helped their populations to recover. They now number in the thousands again, but remain an **endangered** species.

The Great Man-Made River

Many African countries suffer from water shortages. The Libyan government has created a huge river-building project to tackle its water shortages. **Engineers** have drilled into underground stores of water, called **aquifers**, that lie deep under the desert. Water is pumped from these aquifers into the Great Man-Made River— a 2,500-mile (4,000-kilometer) network of pipes that delivers water to Libya's main cities.

Libyans celebrate as they splash in the waters of the Gurdabiya Dam. It is part of Libya's Great Man-Made River Project, the largest engineering project in the world.

Climate change

Africa's greatest environmental challenge is **climate change**. Weather records show that Africa is getting hotter every year. No one knows exactly what this will mean, but the predictions are not good. They include greater water shortages, more **droughts**, and the spread of diseases such as **malaria**. One of the worst-affected places is likely to be the Nile Delta in Egypt. This is one of Africa's main food-producing areas and one of the most populated places on Earth. If climate change causes sea levels to rise, as many experts predict, then much of the Nile Delta could disappear underwater.

AFRICA UP IN SMOKE

A major international report called Africa Up in Smoke included quotes from people who feel that climate change is already affecting them. Here are two views from the report:

"No one is going to survive out here, unless they bring water. I am 70 years old now, and the temperatures are getting hotter and hotter as the years pass by."
Habiba Hassan, Somalia

"I would estimate we now get 40 percent less rain than we used to. Many farmers have left because the water no longer runs along the canal like it used to. These people now have nothing."
Joshua Musyoki-Mutua, Kenya

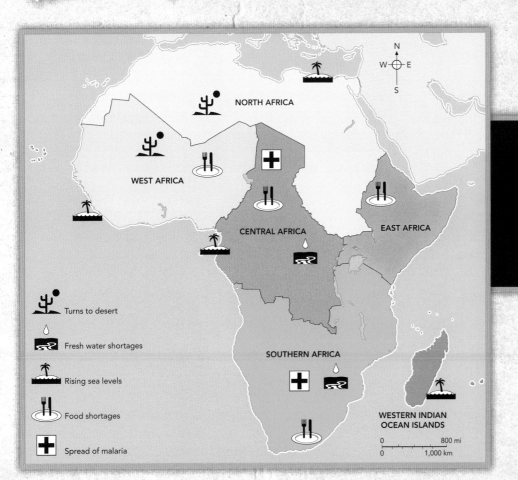

N **W**—**E** **S**

NORTH AFRICA

WEST AFRICA

CENTRAL AFRICA

EAST AFRICA

SOUTHERN AFRICA

WESTERN INDIAN OCEAN ISLANDS

Turns to desert

Fresh water shortages

Rising sea levels

Food shortages

Spread of malaria

0 — 800 mi
0 — 1,000 km

This map shows some of the main ways experts believe Africa might be affected by climate change.

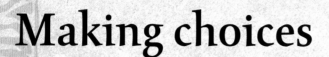

Making choices

Freedom of choice

One of the most important changes for Africa during the 1900s has been greater freedom of choice. African countries became **independent** of their **colonial** masters and formed their own governments. In the early stages, many countries experienced struggles when different groups of people tried to gain control of the new countries. Some of these struggles were violent, and thousands of people died. Today, most African countries are more stable. Their people vote to elect leaders and are able to choose, within reason, where and how they live.

A woman in Sierra Leone casts her vote during an election for a new president in 2007. The right to vote has only come recently to many African people.

Zimbabwean independence

Between 1964 and 1979, Zimbabwe was known as Rhodesia and was ruled by a white minority that made up less than three percent of the population. Zimbabwe only became independent (from the United Kingdom) in 1980. At that time it was one of Africa's most productive countries, and there was great hope for its future. For many years, Zimbabwe made progress in health, education, and its **economy**. Its new president, Robert Mugabe, was seen as one of Africa's great leaders.

Change in Zimbabwe

Beginning in the mid-1990s, however, the government introduced changes that have destroyed much of this progress. The government took away land belonging to white farmers who had settled there when Zimbabwe was a **colony**. The government wanted Zimbabwe to be owned entirely by black people, as it was before colonialism.

At first this plan was popular with many black people, but the white-owned farms created much of Zimbabwe's wealth. When the farmers left, the farms began to fail. Jobs were lost, and less food was produced. To make things worse, much of the land was given to people with connections to the government and not to those most in need.

Crisis

Millions of Zimbabweans now live in hunger and extreme poverty. In 2008, President Mugabe lost the election, but used his power to ignore the result and call for another vote to take place. The police and army were sent to scare people into voting for Mugabe. The opposition party was forced to pull out, and so Mugabe was reelected without any contest.

In 2009 a new prime minister named Morgan Tsvangirai was sworn in to share power with Mugabe. Tsvangirai has promised to stabilize Zimbabwe's economy and end political violence.

Stopping the cheats

Recent elections in Kenya (2007) and Zimbabwe (2008) have been criticized as unfair. They show that **corruption** is still a problem in parts of Africa. Corruption is when people use their position of power to cheat or threaten others who are less powerful.

In several African countries, the police are known for being corrupt. They sometimes arrest people for little reason and demand money to release them again. Many countries have tried to stop such dishonesty. People are encouraged to report corruption, and elections are now closely watched to uncover cheats. Unfortunately, the worst corruption is often among the leaders themselves. This makes it difficult to get rid of it completely.

How corrupt is Africa?

An organization called Transparency International tries to measure corruption around the world. They give countries a score between 1 and 10 based on how corrupt they are—the lower the score, the more corrupt the country. In 2008 only two African countries (Botswana and Cape Verde) had a score of more than five, and African countries made up half of the 30 countries that scored two or less. Somalia had the lowest score in the world, of just one.

BIOGRAPHY:

ARCHBISHOP DESMOND TUTU

Archbishop Desmond Tutu was the chairman of South Africa's Truth and Reconciliation **Commission**. The commission was set up in 1995 to try to heal the suffering that South Africa experienced during almost 50 years of **apartheid**. Bishop Tutu became known for his fairness during the commission. He gave people the chance to forgive the past and build a better, more united future. Since the commission ended in 1998, Archbishop Tutu has been involved in working for peace elsewhere in Africa.

Archbishop Desmond Tutu has become a world spokesperson following his work to bring peace to South Africa. Here, he is speaking in Geneva, Switzerland.

People take charge

Many of the most successful changes in Africa come from local people. Across the **continent**, communities have found ways to improve their own lives and those of others. Some groups have created new ways to earn money by setting up craft **cooperatives** or small businesses. Others have found ways to help those in need, such as people who are disabled or who have **HIV/AIDS**. Communities also have joined forces to improve or protect the environment. The Green Belt Movement in Kenya is an example of this. Its members are mostly women. They campaign to protect Kenya's forests and have planted more than 30 million trees to replace those already damaged.

Members of the Green Belt Movement started by Wangari Maathai meet in Muranga, Kenya.

Biography: Wangari Maathai

Wangari Maathai is the founder of the Green Belt Movement. Since 2002 she has also been part of the Kenyan government. In 2004 Maathai became the first African woman to win the Nobel Peace Prize. She was given the prize for her environmental work and its links with women's rights and peace in Africa.

These girls are pumping water from a well at a school in Sierra Leone. The well is also used by the local community and saves many hours of work. Water collection is one of the many tasks carried out by children across Africa.

Children speak out

Young people play an important role in African society. They collect water and fuel, help on the family farm, care for their brothers and sisters, run errands, and shop for food. By taking on these responsibilities they must make decisions, such as what to buy or where to get wood. Several countries are now recognizing the importance of children's roles. In Uganda, for example, all village councils now have at least one member who is elected by the children to represent their ideas and problems.

33

Working together

Most African nations share a common history of colonialism. Today, many share common challenges such as poverty, disease, and unfair **trade**. In parts of Africa, countries have been cooperating for many years to solve their problems together.

In West Africa, a group of 15 countries known as the Economic Community of West African States (ECOWAS) have been cooperating since 1975. ECOWAS projects include improving transportation and communication links in West Africa. They also support energy, water, and agricultural programs, and help to keep peace. More recently they have begun to cooperate on how to respond to the threat of **climate change**.

African Union

The **African Union (AU)** was formed in 2002 to help Africa overcome its colonial history and create a strong and healthy continent for the 21st century. Most importantly, the African Union is about African nations finding their own solutions to the challenges they face. Many African nations have become dependent on overseas aid to help them solve problems, but in some cases this has led to problems. It has made some countries too dependent on aid. In others, aid money has been stolen because of corruption, or aid has failed because the problems facing Africa have not been properly understood. The AU believes that Africans themselves are the best people to solve the challenges facing the region.

NEPAD

The New Partnership for Africa's Development (NEPAD) was created in 2001 by African leaders and is managed by the African Union. Its main goals are:

- to stamp out poverty

- to begin the successful and lasting development of African countries and the continent

- to stop Africa getting the worst deal in global systems, and help it move fully into the global economy

- to empower (give power to) women faster.

One of the African Union's (AU's) most important jobs is to protect people in areas of conflict. This AU soldier is in the Sudanese village of Kerkera in the troubled Darfur region of Sudan.

The World and Africa

A challenge for us all

Many African countries were in a worse state in 2000 than they had been 20 years earlier. The **Commission for Africa** was set up to investigate this problem. The **commission** talked to important leaders and thousands of ordinary Africans. It asked how the new millennium could be different for Africa, and how the rest of the world could help.

People marched in Edinburgh, the capital of Scotland, in 2005 to persuade world leaders to do something about poverty in Africa and other poor parts of the world. More than 200,000 people took part in the march.

The commission described the difference between the lives of people in rich countries and poor people in Africa as "the greatest scandal of our age." Their report said that as many Africans were dying every month as were killed in the Indian Ocean tsunami of 2004. It described Africa as having a deadly tide of disease and hunger, which is rarely shown on the television news like other disasters. The commission warned that we cannot ignore the situation in Africa just because it is not on television. It said that immediate actions were needed to prevent millions more Africans from dying.

Drop the debt

Many African countries have borrowed money to help pay for development projects, but now struggle to pay these **loans** back and have large **debts**. The money was borrowed from wealthier countries or from international organizations such as the **World Bank**. Unfortunately, the money was not always spent wisely and large amounts were stolen by corrupt leaders. Other money had to be used to buy goods or employ people from the country that gave it. This money is known as **tied aid**.

Forgiving or dropping the debts of Africa's poorest nations is one way that wealthier countries are now planning to help Africa. By 2008 more than $20 billion in debt relief had been promised to 19 of the poorest countries in Africa.

AFRICA FACT
For every $2 that Africa receives in aid, it pays back nearly $1 in debt repayments.

Africa and global trade

Africa's share of global trade is smaller today than it was in the 1980s. Unfair **trade** rules make it hard for African producers to compete. For instance, **subsidies** paid to European and American farmers allow them to sell their produce for less than many African farmers. Schemes such as **fair trade** can help at a local level, but bigger changes will be necessary to help the whole **continent**.

The **World Trade Organisation (WTO)** controls the rules of global trading. African countries asked for a change in these rules to make it fairer for them to compete. The WTO is controlled by a few more powerful countries, such as the United States and members of the European Union. So far they have blocked any changes to the rules of global trade that would benefit Africa.

New trade partners

Historically, African countries have traded mainly with their neighbors and former **colonial** powers. Since 2000 there has been a steady growth in trade between Africa and new regions of the world. One of the most important of these has been increased trade with China. China is the world's most populated country and has one of the fastest-growing **economies** in the world. To help it grow it needs access to Africa's resources. The Chinese government is offering to help many African countries with development projects in return for access to its **resources**.

Not all Chinese trade is good for Africa, though. China has been buying oil from Sudan and there are concerns that some of the money Sudan earns is being used to buy weapons. In other parts of Africa, cheap Chinese goods are now available for sale in local markets. These have been blamed for putting some local companies out of business, because they cannot make goods as cheaply as Chinese companies.

A market in Bobo-Dioulasso, Burkina Faso, sells household goods. Many of these goods now come from China and India instead of being made locally. This is causing some African industries to close down.

Changes Ahead

Despite the progress that Africa has made in the first years of the new millennium, experts say it needs to do more—and fast. Africa's population is still growing quickly and this means that homes, schools, and hospitals are filling up as fast as governments are building them. The environment is also getting worse, and no one is sure what the impact of **climate change** will be. There is still no widely available prevention for **malaria** and there is currently no cure for **HIV/AIDS**. Between them these diseases kill around three million Africans every year.

This clinic in Kenya helps children suffering from malaria. It is visited by American actress and Youth AIDS Global Ambassador Ashley Judd. Africa needs more facilities like this to improve the lives of people living there.

Millennium Development Goals

The Millennium Development Goals (MDGs) were agreed in 2000 and set targets for all nations to reach by the year 2015. These include goals on reducing poverty, providing more education and health care, and improving women's rights. Examples such as Uganda's Universal Primary Education (UPE) program and Kenya's Green Belt Movement are helping to meet some of these goals. As a region, though, Africa is failing to meet them. In 2006 experts said that, at the current rate, meeting the goal of reducing poverty by half would take another 150 years!

Positive examples

Many people hope that greater cooperation between African nations will help the **continent** meet its needs more quickly. The **African Union (AU)** organizes meetings that allow business, political, and community leaders to learn from one another's positive examples. Africa is also trying to improve its image in the wider world. It is true that Africa has many problems, but it also has successful industries and growing **trade** links.

In 2010 South Africa will become the first African nation to host the World Cup soccer finals. Besides the sporting event itself, South Africa is looking forward to showing the world how far it has come since the end of **apartheid** in 1994. It hopes to show the world a changing and positive 21st-century Africa.

Workers construct a new stadium in Johannesburg, South Africa. Some of the 2010 World Cup soccer finals will take place at this stadium. South Africa is the first African nation to host this important sports event.

Timeline

1980   Zimbabwe becomes **independent** from the United Kingdom.

1994   South Africa ends **apartheid**, and Nelson Mandela is elected to be the country's first black leader.

1995   South Africa's Truth and Reconciliation **Commission** begins to repair the damage done by apartheid. It is chaired by Archishop Desmond Tutu and continues working until 1998.

1996   Uganda announces the introduction of its Universal Primary Education (UPE) program. It will pay for up to four children in every family to have free elementary education.

2000   Millennium Development Goals (MDGs) set targets to improve living conditions for the world's poorest countries by the year 2015.

2001   African leaders agree the New Partnership for Africa's Development (NEPAD)—a plan to improve development and reduce poverty across the **continent**.

2002   The **African Union (AU)** is launched as a replacement for the Organization of African Unity (OAU). The AU has 53 member countries.

2004   Wangari Maathai is awarded the Nobel Peace Prize. She is the first African woman to be given the prize, for her work with women and the environment.

2004   The **Commission for Africa** is created. It is made up of 17 international leaders, 9 of whom are African.

2005   The Commission for Africa presents the report Our Common Interest.

2005   The biggest ever anti-poverty movement comes together under the slogan "Make Poverty History."

2005   Leaders of the world's seven richest **economies** (known as the G7) agree to help Africa by forgiving the **debts** of its poorest countries.

2006   Leaders from more than 40 African countries take part in **trade** meetings with China in Beijing.

2007   While G8 leaders meet in Germany for the G8 Summit, thousands of people gather in London, England, for "The World Can't Wait" rally.

2010   South Africa becomes first African nation to host the World Cup soccer finals.

Glossary

African Union (AU) organization of 53 African countries that was launched in 2002 to promote development in the continent

antiretroviral (ARV) drugs used to prolong the life of people with HIV

apartheid system of separation introduced by the white South African government in 1948. Nonwhite people were sent to separate schools, had separate transport, and even separate seats in public spaces. The system ended in 1994.

aquifer underground store of water

brain drain loss of highly skilled workers to other countries

civil war war fought within a country, between different groups

climate change process of the climate changing. Since 1990 changes in the world's climate have been blamed on human activities such as pollution caused by using fossil fuels.

colonial state of being a country that belongs to another country

colony land controlled by another country

commission group of people who are given the responsibility to carry out a certain task

Commission for Africa group of 17 international leaders who explored why Africa was continuing to fall behind the rest of the world and tried to find solutions to its problems

conservation protecting the environment, wildlife, and natural resources from damage

continent one of the main areas of land on Earth. Many countries may be found in one continent.

cooperative organization owned or managed jointly by the people who participate in it

corruption use of power to threaten or cheat others who are less powerful

crop plant grown for use by people, such as cereals or vegetables

debt money owed to an individual or organization

deforestation cutting down of all or most of the trees in a forest. Deforestation can cause environmental damage, including soil erosion and loss of plant and animal species.

desertification process by which land becomes more desertlike and less able to support life

drought when there is little or no rainfall over a long time, causing water shortages and crop damage

economy system under which a country creates, sells, and buys products

endangered animal species that is threatened with extinction

engineer person who uses scientific and mathematical knowledge to find solutions to practical problems such as building, construction, and mining

erosion wearing away of rocks or soil by wind or water

export goods sold to another country; to sell to another country

fair trade trade that makes sure workers are treated fairly and paid a reasonable price for their work and goods

famine severe food shortages causing starvation

fatal causing death

fertile rich in materials or health needed for growth

habitat local environment that is home to particular types of plants and animals

HIV/AIDS the disease AIDS is caused by the HIV virus. The virus attacks the body's ability to protect against infection. There is no cure for HIV or AIDS.

import goods bought by another country; to buy from another country

income money earned through work

independent when a country is free to make its own laws and decisions

infected caught a disease

informal economy part of the economy that is not regulated by the government. People in the informal economy are often working illegally and do not pay taxes.

international community countries of the world which cooperate on issues of global importance

invest put money in to make a profit

life expectancy number of years someone can expect to live, on average

livestock animals kept for use or profit, such as farm animals

loan sum of money lent to another person or country. The person or country must pay the money back within an agreed time and for a specified fee (called interest).

malaria disease that is spread by the bite of mosquitoes

pit latrine simple type of toilet that is a covered pit

poach illegal hunting of animals and wildlife

rain forest thick, forested area in a tropical region that supports a huge range of plants and animals

raw material natural resource before it is processed by machines

remittance money sent back to a home country by people who live and work in other countries

resource mineral or raw material that is used by industries, businesses, and governments to produce goods or services

rural related to life in the country

slum city area characterized by overcrowding and poor living conditions

species particular type of animal or plant

sub-Saharan Africa area of Africa south of the Sahara Desert

subsidy payment made by a government to farmers that encourages them to grow certain types of crop

tax money that the government collects from people and businesses in order to finance the running of the country

tied aid money given to help a country develop, but that has to be used to buy goods or employ people from the country that gave it

trade buy and sell goods

urban related to town or city life

wage money paid to people for the work they do

World Bank international organization that provides funding for countries to spend on development projects such as roads, power supplies, and education

World Trade Organisation (WTO) international organization that sets the rules for global trade and solves disputes between countries who disagree over trade issues

Find Out More

Books

Bowden, Rob. *Africa South of the Sahara*. Chicago, Ill.: Heinemann Library, 2008.

Friedman, Mel. *Africa*. New York, N.Y.: Children's Press, 2009.

Gritzner, Jeffrey A. *North Africa and the Middle East*. New York, N.Y.: Chelsea House, 2006.

Winter, Jeanette. *Wangari's Trees of Peace: A True Story from Africa*. Orlando, Fla.: Harcourt, 2008.

Websites

Africa Aid
www.africaaid.org
This website explains some of the current aid programs in Africa to support health care, education, water, and the **economy**.

BBC World News: Africa
http://news.bbc.co.uk/1/hi/world/africa
The BBC Africa homepage gives information about the latest news and events from the African **continent**.

Office of the Special Advisor on Africa
www.un.org/africa/osaa/
This United Nations website tells about important initiative in Africa, including links to the New Partnership for Africa's Development (NEPAD) and others.

Places to visit

Many museums have good collections of African art and **culture**. Here are some of the more famous ones:

Museum for African Art
36-01 43rd Avenue at 36th Street
Long Island City, NY 11101
Tel: (718) 784-7700
www.africanart.org

National Museum of African Art
Smithsonian Institution
P.O. Box 37012 MRC 708
Washington, DC 20013-7012
Tel: (202) 633-4600
http://africa.si.edu

The Museum of African Culture
13 Brown Street
Portland, ME 04101
Tel: (207) 871-7188
www.africantribalartmuseum.org

Index